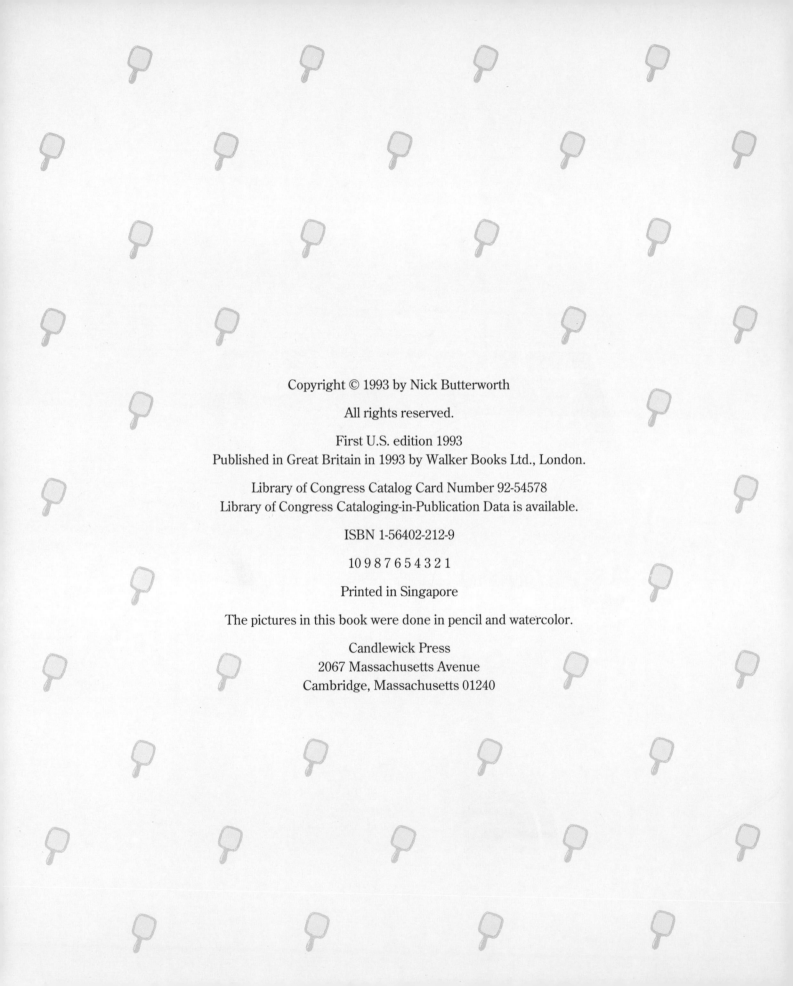

First U.S. edition 1993
Published in Great Britain in 1993 by Walker Books Ltd., London.

Library of Congress Catalog Card Number 92-54578
Library of Congress Cataloging-in-Publication Data is available.

ISBN 1-56402-212-9

10 9 8 7 6 5 4 3 2 1

Printed in Singapore

The pictures in this book were done in pencil and watercolor.

Candlewick Press
2067 Massachusetts Avenue
Cambridge, Massachusetts 01240

MAKING FACES

Written and illustrated by
Nick Butterworth

CANDLEWICK PRESS
CAMBRIDGE, MASSACHUSETTS

Faces, Faces, Faces

Wherever you look you see faces.
People's faces. Animal faces.

Even cars seem to have faces.

The moon has a face. Clocks have faces.
And if you look carefully, you can see faces in
the clouds or in the shapes made by a fire.

Faces are fun to make.
You can draw them, or make model faces.

You can make them with candy
or with fruit or leaves.

But the best way to make faces
is to use your own. So look in the mirror
at the back of this book, and let's
start making faces!

Yucky Medicine

Just imagine, one morning
your mom says to you,
"You don't look very well, dear.
You look all pale and droopy."

🪞 Look in the mirror at your
pale and droopy face.

Then your mom says, "What you
need, dear, is a spoonful of
Dr. Jollis's Strengthening Medicine."

Oh, yuck! You've had it before.
It's green. And lumpy.
It tastes disgusting.
Run and hide. Get on
the couch and look
like a cushion.

🪞 What does your
cushion face
look like?

It's no good. Your mom
has seen you.
Quick! Get under the
table and look like a cat.

 What does your
cat face look like?

Oh, dear! There's no escape.
Here comes your mom.

And here comes a great big spoonful
of Dr. Jollis's green, lumpy
Strengthening Medicine.
Look out!

Oh, yuck! Yucky-yuck!
It tastes disgusting.

What does your
disgusting medicine
face look like?

Snow, Wonderful Snow!

Just imagine a cold, gray winter's day. You're not allowed to play outside. But look out of the window! It's snowing!

What does your face look like when you press it up against the window?

Surely you'll be allowed to play outside now? You ask very nicely. "Please, please, ple-e-e-ease!"

What does your asking nicely face look like?

The answer is yes! You put on your warm clothes and out you go into the yard.

Snow! Wonderful snow! First, you make a few snowballs.

The cat next door is looking worried.

Well, how would you look if
someone much bigger than you
started making snowballs?

You've decided to make
a snow monster.
It's going to be huge
with a great big head.

It's very hard work.
It takes all day.
But at last it's finished.
Suddenly the lady who
lives next door looks
over the fence . . .

What face
does she make
when she sees
your snow monster?

The Moon Man

Just imagine you're flying
to the moon in a spaceship.
It's a dangerous journey.
You have to be serious.

🔍 What does your serious
space pilot face look like?

You're almost there now.
Be careful . . . *Bump!* At last you have landed.
You leave the spaceship to take a look around.

Look out! There's someone
coming. It's a moon man.
You're not scared, are you?

🔍 How do you look when
you're on the moon, and
a moon man comes,
and you're not scared?

The moon man looks sad.
He looks very sad indeed.

🔍 Can you look as sad
as the moon man?

The moon man is sad
because he has no friends.
He lives all alone
on the moon.

Well, that's no problem.
He can fly home with you.
Now he has lots of
friends. He's happy now.

🔍 Can you look
as happy as the
moon man?

Snails and Slugs

Just imagine what it's like being very small, as small as a snail. You have to carry your house on your back and move very slowly.

🪞 Can you make a face like a snail?

Aha! Here come a couple of slugs. They look friendly.

🪞 Can you make a face like a slug?

The slugs don't have nice houses on their backs like you. You must be very proud of your nice house.

🪞 What does your proud face look like?

Oh, no! Here comes a bird.
It's one that eats snails.
You'd better hide inside
your shell.

What face
do you make
for hiding?

It's no good hiding. The bird has a long beak for poking
into shells. You'd better turn back into a person again,
as quickly as you can.

Phlooop! There! The bird is
very surprised. He's amazed.

Can you make an amazed
bird face?

The Fairground

Just imagine a fair.
Peppermint sticks. Cotton
candy. Caramel apples.
You've had one of each.

What does
your sticky face
look like?

The rides are lots of fun.
How about a ride in a plane? You're flying around and
around very fast. Around . . . and around . . . and around
. . . and around. You're getting dizzy.

How do you look when you're dizzy?

Phew! Time for ice cream.
You've chosen a very big cone.
It has three flavors—mmmm!

What face do you make
for delicious?

Now for a ride on the galloping horses.
Hold on tight. You're off! Up and down,
around and around. Up and down,
around and around. Up and down . . .

Oh, dear! Perhaps you
should have had a
smaller cone!

What do you look like when you're feeling sick?

Penguin's Joke

Just imagine these are your friends.
The penguin knows a joke. He thinks it's very funny.
He tells the joke to the rabbit, and the rabbit thinks
it's funny too.

Can you laugh
like the rabbit?

Now the penguin tells the
joke to the bear.
The bear thinks the joke
is funny too.

 Can you laugh
like the bear?

Everyone who hears the joke thinks that it's very funny.

 Can you laugh like them? Like the mouse?
Like the giraffe? Like the robot?

One of your friends whispers the joke to you.
Do you think it's funny? What is the joke? Will you tell?

Visit with Auntie

Just imagine it's Sunday
afternoon and Auntie
is coming over.
Everyone has to look
neat, with faces washed
and hair combed.

What face do you
make when you're
having your hair combed?

Here comes Auntie now.
She's going to give you
a great big wet kiss!
Sssmwwch!
What a kiss!

What face do you
make when Auntie
kisses you?

Auntie sits down.
Oh, dear! Who
left a chocolate
eclair on Auntie's
chair? Auntie
doesn't think
it's funny.
Just look at
her face.

🔍 Can you
make a face
like Auntie's?

Everyone is trying not to laugh,
but it's very hard.

🔍 What do you
look like when
you're trying
not to laugh?

A Boring Day

Just imagine it's a boring
kind of day.
It's raining outside.
You have nothing to do.
Your friend can't come
to play. You're fed up.

How do you look
when you're fed up?

You decide to do some coloring. You're coloring in
a picture of a little cat wearing a big bow tie.
But you keep going over
the lines. It's not your
best coloring, so you
make an angry face
at the cat.

How do you look
when you're angry?

Now you feel really horrible,
so you scribble on the picture.

 Look at your horrible
face in the mirror.

Ding dong! There's someone at the door.
Who is it? Hooray! Your friend has come to play after all.
Even better
than that,
your friend
can spend
the night.
Yippee!

What face
do you make
for yippee?

On the Beach

Just imagine . . . the seashore.
The tide is out and the beach
is wide and flat. And you
have an idea!

You dig the edge of your
shovel into the sand
and start to draw lines.
You whistle as you work.

How do you look
when you whistle?

You're drawing a face. A great, big, long, thin face.

Can you make a face like this one?

What are you drawing now? It's enormous.
It's the biggest, fattest, funniest sand face ever!

Can you make your face look fat and funny?

Oh, dear. The tide is coming in again. The thin face is
getting wet around the eyes. It looks like it's crying.

Can you pretend to cry?

What face do you make?

Don't worry. Next time you come, there'll be
a brand new beach just waiting for you.

In the Jungle

Just imagine you're
exploring the jungle.
It's hot and dark and
a little scary.

What does your
  jungle explorer's
face look like?

There are lots of noises
in the jungle.
Screeches and squawks.
Growls and roars.

Can you make a face
  like a parrot?
    Like a monkey?
      Like a tiger?

You're feeling hungry. So you take out your lunch.
Look out! A huge gorilla is coming toward you.
He looks hungry too. You're afraid he wants to eat you.

🔍 What do you look like when you're afraid?

But the gorilla doesn't want to eat you.
He wants a bite of your banana. Yum!
Now the gorilla is your friend.

🔍 How do you look
   when you're in
the middle of the
jungle sharing a
banana with
a gorilla?

Santa Claus

Just imagine it's Christmas Eve.
You're feeling very excited.

 What does your face
look like on Christmas Eve?

You hang up your stocking and
now it's time for bed. You want
to stay awake to see Santa Claus, but
you're very tired.

 What do you look like
when you're very tired?

Listen!
What's that noise?
It's sleigh bells.
Santa Claus is coming.

You pretend
to be asleep,
but all the
time you keep
peeking out from
under the covers.

What do you look like when you're peeking?

Santa Claus comes into your
room and stands by your bed.
He chuckles to himself.
Do you think he knows
that you're awake?

Santa Claus leaves
a wonderful
present for you.

Look at your face in the mirror. There's the
biggest smile in the whole wide world!